I0664485

# "Penguin Powered Prayer"

Written by Karin E. Schreurs
The 5th & 6th Grade Class 2007-2008
Columbus Christian School

# Penguin Powered Prayer
## Tails of Truth Series
(Schruff Book One)

by Karin E. Schreurs

Genoa, Nebraska
Flower by the Water Publishing

©2008 by Karin E. Schreurs
All Rights Reserved.
No part of this book may be reproduced,
stored in retrieval systems, or transmitted in
any form, by any means, including
mechanical, electronic, photocopying,
recording or otherwise, without prior written
permission of the publisher.

ISBN 978-0-9795805-8-1

Flower by the Water Publishing Company
PO Box 579
Genoa, NE 68640
www.fbwpub.com

Printed in the United States of America

Increasing in wisdom and stature
and in favor with God and men.

Scriptures taken from the American Standard Bible

Dedicated to all God's children who
love to pray!

# Part One:

## Different Kinds of:

## Penguin Powered Prayer

# Penguin Powered Prayer

It is Father God's great pleasure for
you to come. You are His treasure,
His pride and joy to talk to Him as
a daughter or as a son.

### Isaiah 62: 3&4b, 5b
*You will be a crown of beauty in the hand of the Lord.
For the Lord delights in you.  So the Lord will rejoice over
you!*

### I John 3:1a
*See how great a love the Father has bestowed upon us,
that we should be called children of God.*

# <u>Adoration</u> is a type of **Penguin Powered Prayer**

We stand in awe of how great God <u>is</u>
He made the stars, the sea, and the land.
All the fullness of the earth is <u>His</u>!

**Psalm 24:1**
*The earth is the Lord's and all it contains, the world and those who dwell in it. For He has founded it upon the seas and established it upon the rivers.*

**Psalm 96:4**
*For great is the Lord and greatly to be praised!*

# <u>Praise</u> is a type of
# Penguin Powered Prayer

Let everyone who has breath praise the
<u>Lord</u>!
Praise Him with instruments and singing
from one generation to generation in one
<u>accord</u>!

### Psalm 78:4-7
*We will not conceal them from their children, but tell to the generation to come the praises of the Lord and His strength and His wondrous work that He has done.*

### Psalm 150:3-6
*Praise Him with trumpet sound, harp and lyre, with tambourine*
*and dancing, with stringed instruments*
*and pipe and with loud cymbals;*
*Let everything that has breathe praise the Lord!*

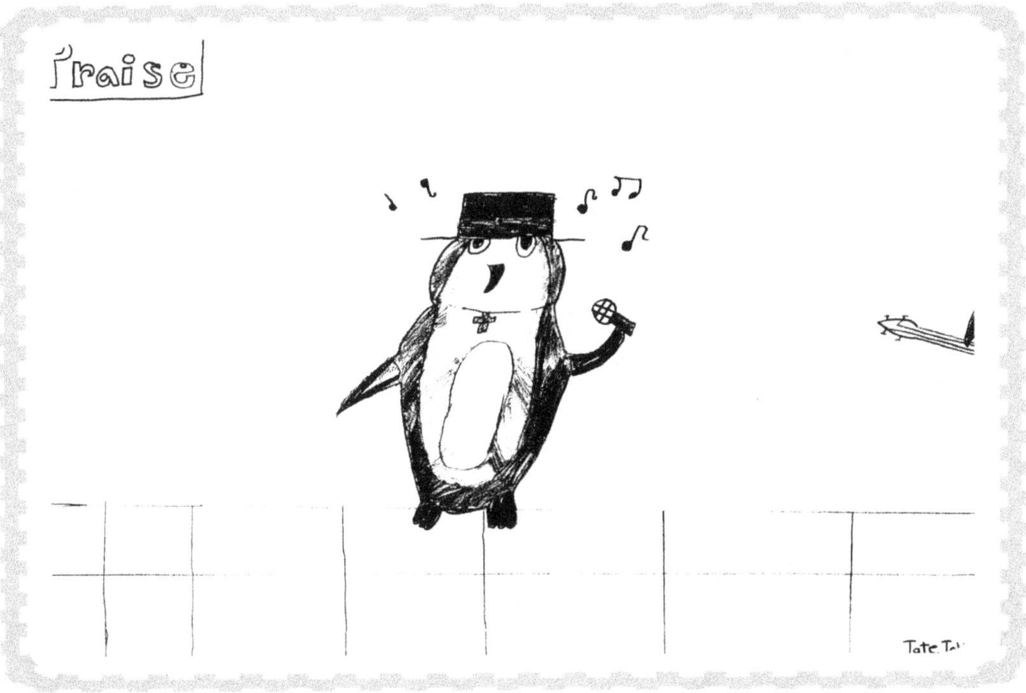
Praise
Tate T.

# <u>Consecration</u> is a type of Penguin Powered Prayer

Lord I give my entire self to <u>You</u>
My thoughts, words, and actions Oh Lord
Every day clean me and use me,
for Your glory <u>too!</u>

### Psalm 25:1
*"Unto You, O Lord, do I bring my life."*

### Romans 12: 1
*By the mercies of God, to present your bodies a living and holy sacrifice, acceptable to God, which is your spiritual service of worship.*

# **Confession** is a type of
# **Penguin Powered Prayer**

To repent of sin and go the other <u>way</u>
By asking God to search our hearts and
actions
To clean us from the inside out we <u>pray.</u>

**Psalm 51:2**

*Wash me thoroughly from my iniquity and cleanse me from my sin.*

**I John 1:9**

*If we confess our sins, He is faithful and righteous to forgive us our sins and to cleanse us from all unrighteousness.*

# The Prayer of **Commitment** is a type of **Penguin Powered Prayer**

Give God all your problems and pressures of life. Let God work out everything in His time There is no need to be worried or be full of strife.

**Psalm 37:5**

*Commit your way to the Lord, trust also in Him and He will do it.*

**I Peter 5:7**

*Casting all your cares upon Him, because He cares for you.*

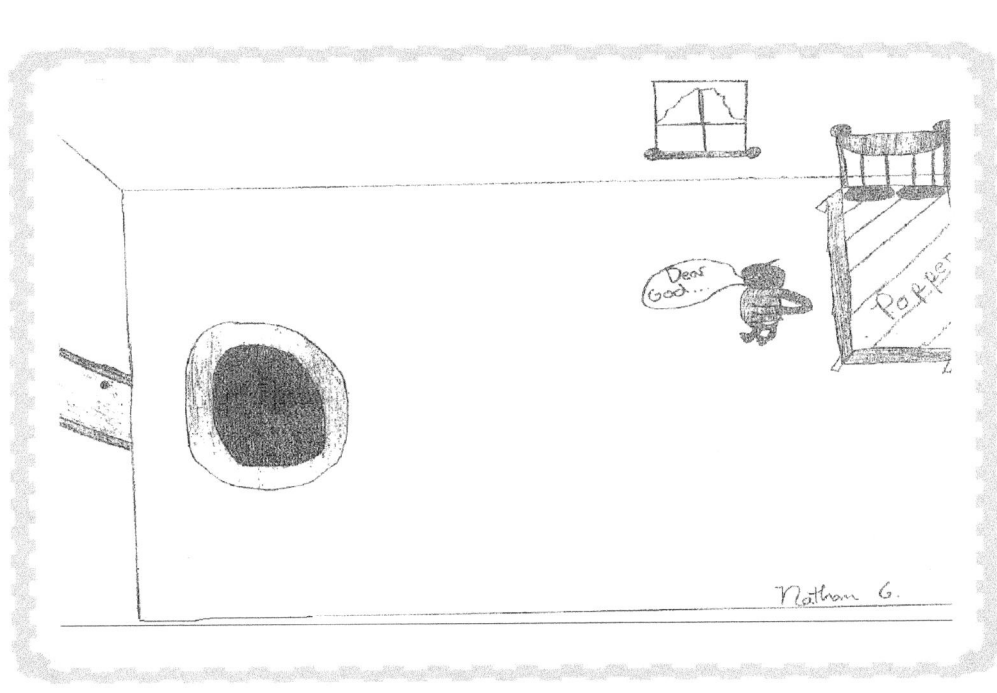

# <u>Thanksgiving</u> is a type of
# Penguin Powered Prayer

Thank you Lord, for all you <u>do</u>!
You supply our daily needs,
food, family, friends, and houses <u>too</u>!

### Psalm 9:1
*I will give thanks to the Lord with all my heart; I will tell of all Thy wonders!*

### Psalm 26:7
*That I may proclaim with the voice of thanksgiving and declare all Thy wonders!*

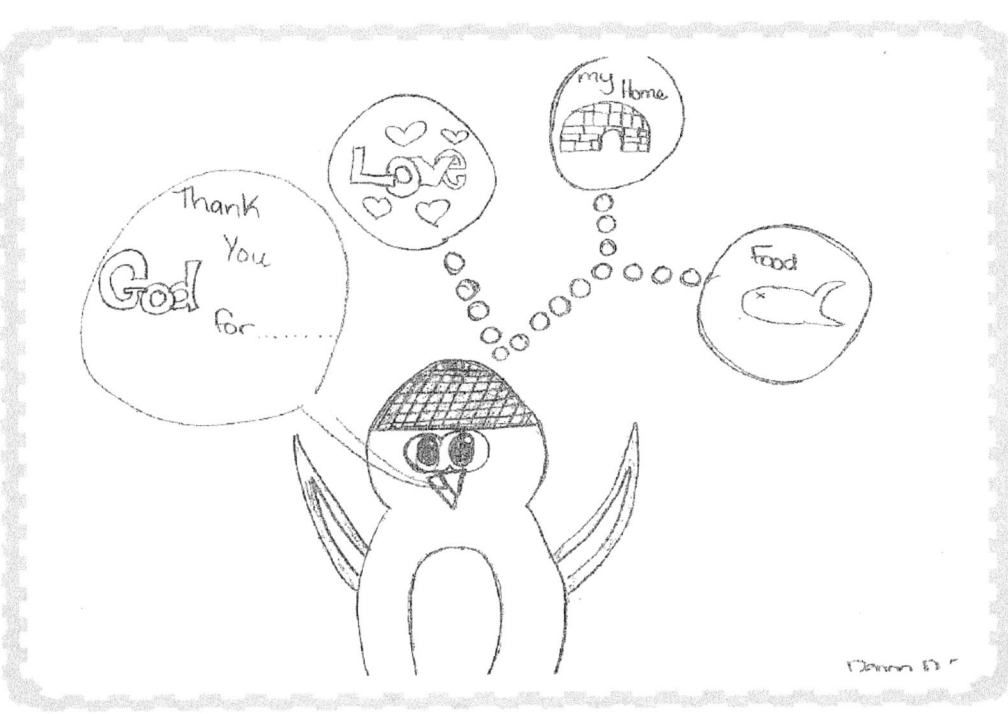

# Petitions for others
## are a type of
## Penguin Powered Prayer

To ask God to bless those who are
in need this very <u>hour</u>
Those who feel afraid, sad, or sick,
Lord, touch them with Your Mighty <u>Power!</u>

**Psalm 20: 5b**
*May the Lord fulfill all your petitions.*

**Matthew 6: 13b**
*For Thine is the kingdom and the power and the glory
forever, amen!*

# <u>Petition</u> for self
## is a type of
## Penguin Powered Prayer

Asking God for the desires of your <u>heart</u>
Knowing God's will and purpose we trust
Him
His loving kindness will never <u>depart!</u>

**Matthew 7:7**
*Ask and it shall be given to you, seek and you shall find,
knock and it shall be opened to you. Forever one who asks
receives and he who seeks finds, and to him who knocks it
shall be opened.*

**Psalm 37:4**
*Delight yourself in the Lord and He will give you the desires
of your heart.*

# Speaking **God's Word**
## is a type of
# Penguin Powered Prayer

Speaking the Bible, God's promises
are <u>true</u> God's Holy Angels move and
minister
to His children.  Amen- giving God all
the
glory in all that He can <u>do!</u>

**John 15:7**
*"If you abide in Me and My words abide in you, ask
whatever
you wish and it shall be done for you."*

**Psalm 103:20**
*Bless the Lord you His angels, mighty in strength, who
perform
His Word, obeying the voice of His Word!*

# The Prayer of
## **<u>Perseverance</u>**
## is a type of
## **Penguin Powered Prayer**

Continue to pray as God leads <u>you</u>
until you see the answer fulfilled
for the situation.
Never give up, God's promises are <u>true</u>.


**Luke 18: 1 & 7**
*Now He was telling them a parable to show that at*
*all times they ought to pray  and not to lose heart.*
*God brings justice for His elect, who cry to Him day and*
*night.*


**Galatians 6:9**
*And let us not lose heart in doing good,*
*for in due time we shall reap if we do not grow weary.*

# Prayers of **Agreement**
# are a type of
# **Penguin Powered Prayer**

When we join our faith with two or three
and pray together
Humbly praying, God's will to be done
And saying Amen! with our sister and
brother.


**Matthew 18:19-20**
*If two of you agree on earth about anything that they may ask,
it shall be done for them by My Father who is in heaven.
For where two or three have gathered together in
My name, there I am in their midst.*


**James 4:10**
*Humble yourselves in the presence of the Lord and He will
exalt you.*

# <u>Supplication</u> is a type of Penguin Powered Prayer

Do not fear or feel all <u>alone</u>
Call upon the Lord and draw near to Him
God will hear your voice from His Holy <u>throne.</u>

**Psalm 145:18**
*The Lord is near to all who call upon Him;*
*to all who call upon Him in truth.*

**Psalm 6:9**
*The Lord has heard my supplication, the Lord receives my prayers.*

# <u>Worship</u> is a type of Penguin Powered Prayer

Come and bow down before your <u>maker</u>
be still and know that He is God
in His presence is joy; our heavenly
<u>Father</u>.

**Psalm 95:6&7**

*Come let us worship and bow down; let us kneel
before the Lord our maker.  For He is our God.*

**John 4:23**

*"But an hour is coming and now is when  the true
worshippers
shall worship the Father in spirit and truth; for such people
the Father seeks to be His worshippers."*

# The **sinner's prayer** is a type of **Penguin Powered Prayer**

Forgive me Lord, I believe that
Jesus died for <u>me</u>
He took my sins upon Himself.
Come into my heart, into my life,
thank you for setting me <u>free!</u>

**Romans 3:23**

*For all have sinned and fall short of the glory of God.*

**Romans 10:9&10**

*That if you confess with your mouth Jesus as Lord and believe in your
heart that God raised Him from the dead you shall be saved.*

# <u>Pray for your enemies</u> is
## a type of
## Penguin Powered Prayer

Even for those who have treated you <u>wrong</u>
don't try to "get even" with them
God says to bless them with your <u>tongue</u>.

**Matthew 5:44**

*"But I say to you, love your enemies, and pray for those who persecute you."*

**Luke 6:27 & 28**

*"But I say to you who hear, love your enemies, do good to those
who hate you, bless those who curse you, pray for those who mistreat you."*

# The **<u>prayer of faith</u>**
## is a type of
## Penguin Powered Prayer

To arise and believe God's promises are
<u>true</u>
It is a gift from God that comes from
your heart
Ask in Jesus Name and it will be given
unto <u>you</u>!

**Romans 5:1**
*Therefore, having been justified by faith, we have peace with
God through our Lord Jesus Christ.*

**Matthew 9:29**
*"Be it done to you, according to your faith"*

# Penguin Powered Prayer

It is the Father's will for His children
to experience answered <u>prayer</u>
To receive His wisdom, strength, and
authority
and to understand His great love and His
wonderful <u>care</u>.


**Matthew 16:19**
*"I will give you the keys of the Kingdom of heaven."*


**Ephesians 3: 19 & 20**
*And to know the love of Christ which surpasses knowledge,*
*that you may be fill up to the fullness of God. Now to Him*
*who is able to do*
*exceeding abundantly beyond all that we ask or think,*
*according to*
*the power that works within us.*

# Penguin Powered Prayer

Thy Kingdom come, Thy will be <u>done</u>
on earth as it is in heaven above
to God be the Glory, in Jesus name, we
<u>come!</u>

**Matthew 7:10**
*Thy Kingdom come, Thy will be done,
on earth as it is in heaven.*

**Matthew 7:13**
*For Thine is the Kingdom and the power and
the glory, forever. Amen!*

# Penguin Powered Prayer

So, be strong in the Lord and in the
power of His <u>might</u>.
Pray at all times on every occasion, in
every season.
For God's will to be done on earth,
bringing forth His <u>light!</u>

**Ephesians 6:10 & 18b**
*Be strong in the Lord and in the strength of His might.*
*Pray at all time in the Spirit.*

**Isaiah 60:1**
*Arise shine, for your light has come, and the*
*glory of the Lord has risen upon you!*

# Part Two:

*Terror*

PRAYER

# Keys to:
# Penguin Powered Prayer

## Humility inherits powerful
## Penguin Powered Prayer

They have everything to do with the attitude of
the <u>heart</u>

They are simple sincere, not rules and
regulations

A relationship with God, never to <u>depart.</u>

## I Samuel 16:7
*...man looks at the outward appearance, but the Lord looks
at the heart.*

## Matthew 5:5
*Blessed are the humble, for they shall inherit the earth.*

# Obedience Obtains Penguin Powered Prayer

It excels when we take time to listen and <u>obey</u>
God's direction for each of our lives
and a desire to please Him in every <u>way</u>.

**I John 3:22**

*And whatever we ask we receive from Him, because we keep
His commandments and do the things that are pleasing in His
sight.*

**Ephesians 6:1-3**

*Children obey your parents in the Lord, for this is right.
Honor your
father and mother.   That it may be well with you, and that
you may live long on the earth.*

# Obedience

It excels when we take time to listen and obey God's direction for each of our lives and a desire to please Him in every

1 John 3:22

Hebrews 11:8

By: Nicole

# Proper Submission Profits Penguin Powered Prayer

Happen when a person submits to <u>authority</u>
Their parents, grandparents, pastors, and
teachers
Listening and serving with joy and <u>humility</u>

**Hebrews 13:17**
*Obey your leaders and submit to them; for they keep
watch over your souls, as those who will
give an account. Let them to this with joy and not with grief.*

**Proverbs 28:9**
*He who turns away his ear from listening to the law,
even his prayer is an abomination (not worthy).*

# Compassion & Caring Creates
# Penguin Powered Prayer

When we care and focus more for <u>others</u>
Giving them honor, kindness, and respect
to our sisters and brothers, and even to
<u>strangers</u>.

## Galatians 6:10
*While we have opportunity, let us do good to all men
and especially to those who are of the household of the faith.*

## I Peter 2:17
*Honor all men; love the brotherhood, fear God, honor the
king.*

## Forgiveness is foundational for Penguin Powered Prayer

Forgive those who have hurt you this very <u>hour</u>
Forgiveness is something we don't do by feelings
It is a decision of our will, by God's grace and <u>power</u>.

### Mark 11:25

*And whenever you stand praying, forgive, if you have anything*
*against anyone; so that your Father also who is in heaven may*
*forgive you your transgressions.*

### Matthew 18:21 & 22

*"Lord, how often shall my brother sin against me and*
*I forgive him? Up to seven times? Jesus said to him, "I do*
*not say to you,*
*up to seven times, but up to seventy times seven."*

## Faith Expects Penguin Powered Prayer

Have faith in God's awesome <u>ability</u>
Don't give up, but hope in God!
Believe and receive His peace and <u>stability</u>.

## Hebrews 11:1
*Now faith is the assurance of things hoped for, the conviction of things not seen.*

## Mark 11:22
*And Jesus answered saying to them, " Have faith in God."*

**Love Releases Penguin Powered Prayer**

Comes by walking daily in God's holy light from
<u>above</u>
In Jesus, receiving and giving faith, hope, and
love,
but the greatest of these is <u>love!</u>

### Ephesians 5:2

*And walk in love, just as Christ also loved you and gave
Himself up for us, an offering and a sacrifice to
God as a fragrant aroma.*

### I Corinthians 13:13

*But now abide faith, hope, love, these three;
but the greatest of these is love.*

# Part Three
## Hook Ups to: **Penguin Powerless Prayer**

# Penguin Powerless Prayer

# Sin produces Penguin Powerless Prayer

If I have sin hidden in my <u>heart</u>
I can't pray with confidence
There is no open communication to <u>start</u>

## Psalms 66:18
*If I regard wickedness in my heart, the Lord will not hear.*

## Psalms 24:3
*Who may ascend into the hill of the Lord?  And who may stand in His holy place?  He who has clean hands and a pure heart.*

**Doubt** and **unbelief** will fall into
Penguin Powerless Prayer

Satan will try to fill our minds with questions
The "what if" or "it won't"
We get distracted and don't learn from our lessons.

**James 1:6**
*But let him ask in faith without any doubting, for the one
who doubts is like the surf of the sea driven and tossed by the
wind .*

**James 1:7**
*For let not that man expect that he will receive anything
from the Lord.*

**Worry** will weigh you down to
**Penguin Powerless Prayer**

The sin of worry is a "disease" in many <u>ways</u>
Don't be anxious about today or tomorrow
Put your trust in God for all your <u>days</u>

**Matthew 6:34**
*"Therefore do not be anxious for tomorrow;*
*for tomorrow will care for itself.*

**I Peter 5:7**
*Casting all your anxiety upon Him, because He cares for*
*you.*

## **Un-forgiveness** ties knots with
## **Penguin Powerless Prayer**

Holding grudges causes inward <u>pain</u>
Can there ever be enough payback?
Anger and resentment, holding on to <u>blame</u>

### **Romans 12: 19**
*Never take your own revenge, beloved, but leave room*
*for the wrath of God, for it is written,*
*"Vengeance is Mine, I will repay, says the Lord.*

### **Ephesians 4:26 & 27**
*Be angry and yet do not sin; do not let the sun go down on*
*your anger,*
*and do not give the devil an opportunity.*

God please help me to forgive Chuck

**Pride** pours out **Penguin Powerless Prayer**

"I can do it myself" or "I'll do it my way,"
boasting and self-reliance causes trouble.
Repent, and ask God to help you each day!

**I Peter 5:5b**
*God is opposed to the proud, but gives grace to the humble.*

**Proverbs 16:18**
*Pride goes before destruction*

**Negative Words** cut and leads to
**Penguin Powerless Prayer**

Your words can agree with God's <u>promises</u>
Or they can stop the blessings of God
There is no room for <u>compromises.</u>

**Proverbs 18:21**
*Death and life are in the power of the tongue.*

**James 1:26**
*If any one thinks himself to be religious, and yet
does not bridle his tongue but deceives his own heart,
this man's religion is worthless.*

## Lack of Gratitude multiplies
## Penguin Powerless Prayer

When you murmur, grumble, and complain
You are never satisfied for what you do have
Instead, be thankful and God's peace will
remain.

### Philippians 2:14
*Do all things without grumbling or disputing.*

### Philippians 2:8 & 9 (parts)
*Whatever is true, honorable, right, pure, lovely, good repute,
let your mind dwell and practice on these thing
and the God of peace shall be with you.*

# Lack of Gratitude

# ABC's of Penguin Powered Prayer

A. Admit you are a sinner... *"for all have sinned and fall short of the glory of God."* Romans 3:10, 23 Romans 5:8, 6:23

B. Believe in Jesus... *"For God so loved the world that he gave his only Son, that whoever believes in Him shall not perish, but have Eternal Life."* John 3:16, John 4:6

C. Confess that Jesus is your Lord... *"If you confess with your mouth, 'Jesus is Lord' and believe in your heart that God raised Him from the dead, you will be saved."* Romans 10:9&10

# Penguin Powered Promises

## God's Will

Psalm 32:8
Psalm 23:3
John 10:3&4

## Peaceful Sleep

Psalm 127:2b
Proverbs 3:24

## Fear Not

Psalm 27:1
II Timothy 1:7
Joshua 1:9

## Protection

Psalm 91:11
II Samuel 22:2&3
Romans 10:17

## Faith

Mark 11:22
Luke 17:5
Isaiah 53:5
Hebrews 12:2

## Healing

Psalm 147:3
James 5:16

## Repent

Mark 1:15
Acts 2:38

## Forgiveness

Mark 2:7
I John 1:19

## Father's Love

I John 3:1
John 3:16

Columbus Christian School
P.O. Box 924
Columbus, NE 68602-0924
402-562-6470

We pray that you enjoyed reading the book:

"Penguin Powered Prayer"

Mrs. Schreurs

And the

5th & 6th Grade Class at CCS.

*Taylor Engel*
*Aiden Schneider*

*Ashley Nicole Hamlings*

*Zachary*

*Bela*

*Tate R. Tobiason*

*Mrs. Schreurs*

*Casey Christensen*

*David E Jones*

*Brandon*
*Brock*

*Shianne Chiappetta*

*Hannah M. Autry*

*David Poffe*

*Nathan J. Griess*

*Amber*   *Nicole Wieberdink*   *Denon D.*   *Teagin*   *Cortney D.*

www.ingramcontent.com/pod-product-compliance
Lightning Source LLC
Chambersburg PA
CBHW080835250626
47160CB00008B/2946